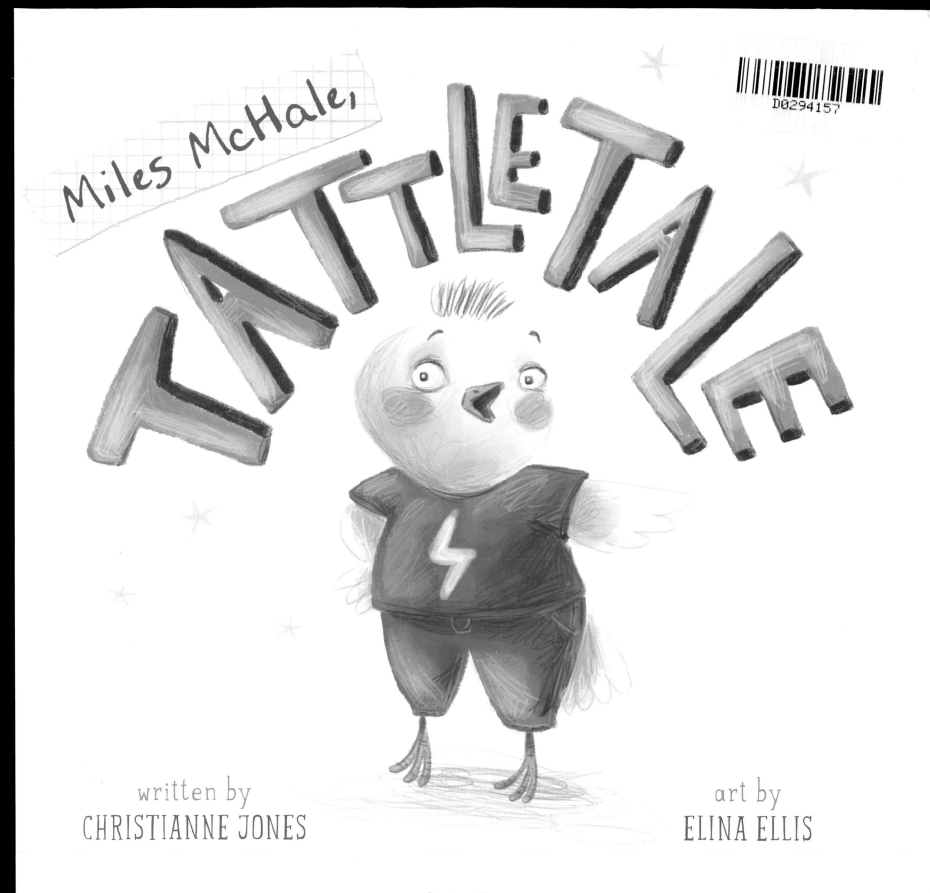

Miles McHale, TATTLETALE

written by
CHRISTIANNE JONES

art by
ELINA ELLIS

Curious Fox
a capstone company-publishers for children

D0294157

First published in 2016 by Curious Fox,
an imprint of Capstone Global Library Limited,
264 Banbury Road, Oxford, OX2 7DY –
Registered company number: 6695582
www.curious-fox.com

Copyright © Curious Fox
The author's moral rights are hereby asserted.
Illustrations by Elina Ellis

All characters in this publication are fictitious
and any resemblance to real persons, living or dead,
is purely coincidental.

ISBN 978 1 78202 833 8
21 20 19 18 17
10 9 8 7 6 5 4 3 2 1

A CIP catalogue for this book is available from the British Library.

All rights reserved.
No part of this publication may be reproduced in any form or by any means
(including photocopying or storing it in any medium by electronic means
and whether or not transiently or incidentally to some other use of this publication)
without the written permission of the copyright owner.

Printed and bound in India.

Designed by Aruna Rangarajan

To Emma, Allie, Thomas, Nolan, Kale, Elsa,
Adalyn, and Landon. Don't be tattletales. — CJ

To my darling boy, Sasha Ellis. — Elina Ellis

Miles McHale was smart.
He was funny. He was sweet.

But Miles McHale was also a **TATTLETALE** –
and not just a one-or-two-times-a-day tattler.

We're talking about **CONSTANT** tattling, all day long.

Sometimes, the tattling didn't even stop at bedtime.

The tattling was a problem at home.

But it was a BIG problem at school.

And Miles wasn't the only tattler.
(But he was the **worst** one.)
So one day, Mrs Snitcher started the

TATTLE BATTLE.

"Okay, class. The rules are simple:
two teams, one week, no tattling.

Whichever team has the fewest
number of tattles gets
EXTRA PLAYTIME on Friday,"
Mrs Snitcher said.

When the teams were assigned,
Miles didn't stop tattling.

"Ava is being too loud!"

"Lola won't stop clapping!"

"Jonathan is standing
on one foot!"

His team was NOT impressed.

"Miles, hold on a minute," Mrs Snitcher said. "Before we start, let's recite the **TATTLE BATTLE PLEDGE.**"

If a friend is sick, hurt, or in harm's way, then telling someone is OKAY.

And with that, the Tattle Battle
officially began.

Miles knew the rules and he didn't want to let his team down. But sometimes it was hard to know what was tattling and what wasn't.

Mrs Snitcher! Allie is chewing on her pencil!

"Is she sick or hurt or in danger?" Mrs Snitcher asked.

"Well . . . she could choke on it," Miles replied.

"True. But that's not likely."

"Okay," Miles said. "Got it."

"Is she sick or hurt or in danger?"
Mrs Snitcher asked.

"Well . . . she might
catch a cold," Miles said.

"Maybe. But that's not likely."

"Okay," Miles said. "Got it."

But he didn't really get it.

He tried hard, but Miles kept letting his team down.
By the end of the week, he found himself alone.

Alone at playtime.

Alone at lunch.

And alone on his walk home.

Nobody wanted to talk to him — especially his teammates. His team was losing the tattle battle and it was all his fault.

"That's it," he said to himself.

"No more tattling. EVER. "

That night, Miles was playing in his room when he heard a loud crash. It sounded like it came from the kitchen.

"Hattie, what happened?" Miles asked.

"I wanted another cookie," his sister said. "But when I climbed onto the counter, I slipped."

Miles had a choice to make. Should he tell his mum or not? He didn't want to be a tattletale, but Hattie was hurt.

Then Miles remembered the **TATTLE BATTLE** pledge:

If a friend is sick, hurt, or in harm's way, then telling someone is OKAY.

The next day, the class recited the Tattle Battle pledge right after the first bell.

If a friend is sick, hurt, or in harm's way, then telling someone is okay.

But at the end of the pledge, Miles McHale went on:

Unless it's sickness, danger, or bullying I see, I will mind my own business and worry about me.

"Miles McHale! That is a wonderful addition to our pledge!" Mrs Snitcher said. "I will take away three tattle points for your team."

Miles **beamed** with pride. His team still lost the Tattle Battle, but that was okay. He apologized to his team and won back his friends.

After that day Miles McHale never tattled
again. In fact, nobody ever tattled again.
Life was perfect.

THE END.

Well ... not quite. But
I did tattle A LOT less
and so did my
friends.